Barkus
Dog Dreams

BOOK 2

BY PATRICIA MACLACHLAN · ILLUSTRATED BY MARC BOUTAVANT

chronicle books·san francisco

For Aisling, and in memory of Casey and Scottie. —Love, P. M.

Text © 2018 by Patricia MacLachlan.
Illustrations © 2018 by Marc Boutavant.

Library of Congress Cataloging-in-Publication Data

Names: MacLachlan, Patricia, author. | Boutavant, Marc, illustrator.
Title: Dog dreams / by Patricia MacLachlan ; illustrated by Marc Boutavant.
Description: San Francisco : Chronicle Books, [2018] | Series: Barkus ; book 2 | Summary:
Barkus is a large and very clever dog, and Baby is a cat, and together their adventures make
life exciting for seven-year-old Nicky and her family.
Identifiers: LCCN 2017045066 | ISBN 9781452116761 (alk. paper)
Subjects: LCSH: Dogs—Juvenile fiction. | Cats—Juvenile fiction. | Families—Juvenile fiction. |
CYAC: Dogs—Fiction. | Cats—Fiction. | Family life—Fiction.
Classification: LCC PZ7.M2225 Do 2018 | DDC [E]—dc23 LC record available at https://lccn.loc.gov/2017045066

ISBN 978-1-4521-1676-1

Manufactured in China.

Design by Sara Gillingham Studio.
Typeset in Harriet and Lunchbox.

10 9 8 7 6 5 4 3 2 1

Chronicle Books LLC
680 Second Street, San Francisco, California 94107
Chronicle Books—we see things differently. Become part of our community at www.chroniclekids.com.

CONTENTS

WHAT BABY FOUND

Barkus was quiet.

He didn't eat his food.

He didn't play with Baby.

He just lay behind the

couch.

"Barkus looks sad," I said.

"Barkus looks sick,"
said my mother.

My father called the vet.
"She says to bring Baby,
too. She is due for a shot."

Barkus lay on the backseat of the car. He didn't sit up and make dog nose smudges on the window.

Baby sat in her cat carrier, looking at Barkus.

Barkus wagged his tail a bit when we got to the vet's clinic. He liked Robin the vet.

Robin sat down on the floor next to Barkus. He didn't try to lick Robin's face the way he always did.

Robin looked in his ears.

"I think Barkus has an ear infection," she said. "He's going to need to take some pills."

Robin taught my father how to give Barkus his pills.

She put the pill in some cheese and opened Barkus's mouth. She held his mouth shut. After a minute Barkus swallowed.

"Bring him back next week," she said.

Then Robin took Baby out of her carrier and gave her a shot.

Baby didn't care. She jumped out of Robin's arms and ran over to be with Barkus.

"Friends," said Robin with a smile.

Every day, my father wrapped the pills in bread, or cheese, or turkey, or ham, or peanut butter.

Every day Barkus took his pills, then went behind the couch.

Then one day he came out from behind the couch.

Soon Barkus wagged his tail at me.

He played with Baby.

Barkus was better! The pills had worked!

But Baby surprised us. She batted Barkus's pills out from behind the couch!

"That's a week of pills!" said my mother.

"Barkus didn't swallow any," I said.

It was time to take Barkus back to the vet.

Barkus sat and looked out the window, his nose on the glass.

He was happy to see Robin.

She looked at one ear, then the other.

"You're all better, Barkus," she said.

"But he didn't take the pills," I said. "Baby found them behind the couch."

Robin laughed. "I guess Barkus got better without them," she said.

She led him to the scale.

"He gained weight while he was sick! How could that happen?" she said.

"I know how it happened," said my mother. "Ham and turkey and bread and cheese . . ."

"And peanut butter," I said. "Barkus likes peanut butter much better than pills."

"He likes peanut butter better than everything," said my mother.

Barkus wagged his tail and whirled around, excited. He barked.

"I think Barkus said 'peanut butter,'" said Robin.

"He did," I said.

"No more peanut butter, Barkus," said Robin. "You'll get fat."

Barkus didn't care.
He licked Robin's
face anyway.

A HIGH NOTE

It was the town's birthday. We carried a picnic basket and a blanket to the park. Barkus walked beside me.

There were sparklers. There were balloons. I opened the dog park gate, and Barkus ran inside. There were many dogs playing.

Ben with short legs—

Rudy, the terrier

who needed brushing—

Molly, the Great Pyr—

Ollie with curls.

A band played a peppy song.

Barkus stopped playing and listened.

Barkus watched.

"Barkus wants to play in the band," I said.

"That's one thing Barkus can't do," said my father.

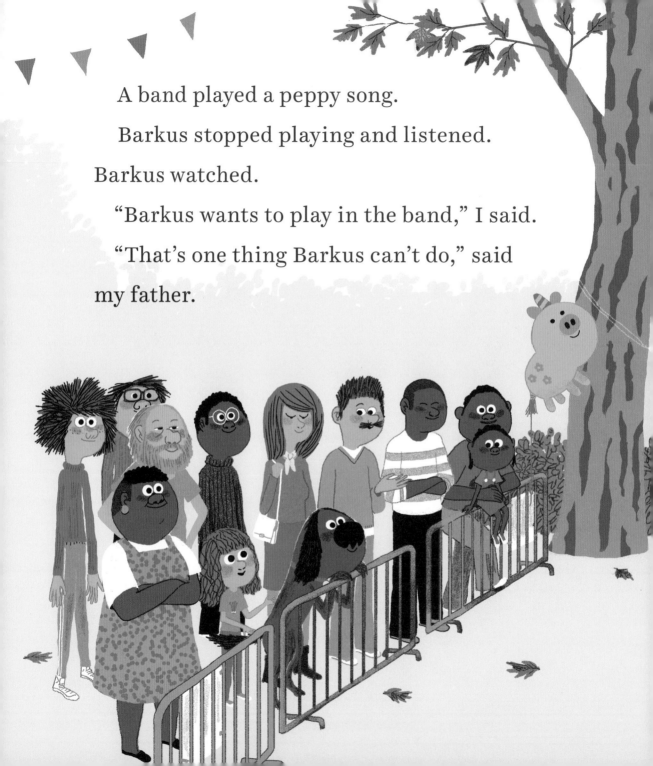

Next, four girls danced onstage. Barkus perked up his ears. He wagged his tail.

"Barkus wants to dance," I said.

"Too bad," said my mother. "That's another thing Barkus can't do."

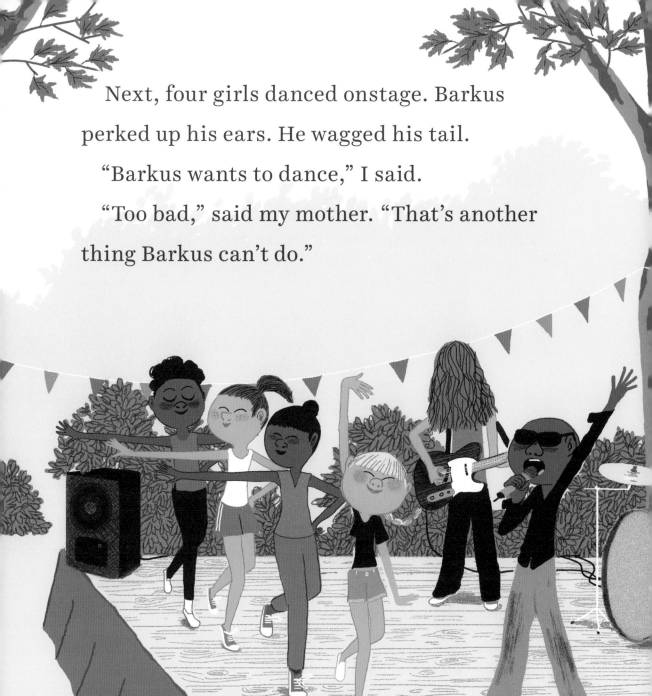

"Catch that balloon!"

a man shouted.

Barkus leaped up and caught
the string in his mouth.

"Thank you, thank you!" said the man.

He handed the balloon to a little girl.

She patted Barkus.

"Good catch," said the man. "That's a good dog."

"The best dog in the world," I said. "That's something Barkus *can* do."

But we would all be surprised.

There was one more thing Barkus could do.

A lady in a fancy dress came onto the stage.

The band conductor lifted his baton.

The band played.

The lady sang.

Then she coughed.

She sneezed.

"Uh-oh," said my father. "She'll never hit the high note at the end of the song."

The lady sang on.

She coughed again. She sneezed twice.

And then came the end of the song.

The lady couldn't reach the high note.

But *someone* could.

Beside me Barkus stood, his nose in the air, his mouth in a little O.

Everyone turned to see where the high note was coming from.

"It's that dog!" someone called.

"A dog?!"

Barkus held the note for so long I finally patted him.

"You can stop, Barkus," I said.

Barkus stopped.

Everyone clapped. Even Mrs. Fillmore clapped.

"And there's another thing Barkus *can* do," I told my mother and father.

The next day there was a picture of Barkus in the newspaper. Under the picture was written:

BARKUS HITS A
HIGH NOTE.

THE VERY LONG DAY

KNOCK, KNOCK, KNOCK!!

It was very early when someone pounded at the front door.

It was Jen who had a farm down the road.

"Where's your father, Nicky?" she asked.

"In bed," I said. "You're wearing pajamas."

"My herd's gone!" said Jen.

My father came out of his bedroom. He was wearing pajamas, too.

"What do you mean *gone*?" he asked.

Barkus padded out from my bedroom. Baby came, too.

"When I got up this morning the fence was broken. Seven cows and two goats are gone. And Bibi, too."

"Who's Bibi?" asked my father.

"Her donkey." I said.

Barkus's ears perked up. Barkus liked Bibi.

My father got his wallet and car keys.

"We'll be back," he said. "When your mother wakes up, tell her where we've gone."

Barkus and Baby went out the door, too.

They were happy outside.

I was happy to go back to bed.

"Nicky!"

It was my mother's voice.

I sat up in bed.

"Where's your father?"

"He went to help Jen find her lost herd."

"Where are Barkus and Baby?"

"I'll find them," I said.

But they weren't outside.

They weren't inside.

They weren't anywhere.

Suddenly we heard noises in the yard.

Barkus was there! Baby was there!
And so were seven cows, two goats with
bells around their necks, and Bibi. There was
a white chicken, too.

My father's car screeched to a halt in front of the house. My father and Jen got out of the car.

"Oh, thank you all!" said Jen. "We couldn't find them anywhere."

"It wasn't me," said my mother.

"It wasn't me," I said. "It was Barkus and Baby."

"Barkus and Baby?" said my father.

"You have your pajamas on," said my mother.

"Where did the chicken come from?" asked Jen.

"Isn't it your chicken?" asked my mother.

"Nope," said Jen. "But I'll take her home."

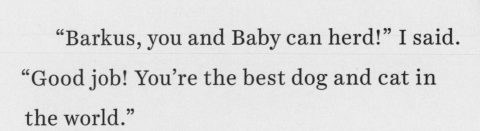

"Barkus, you and Baby can herd!" I said.

"Good job! You're the best dog and cat in
the world."

"You are!" said Jen.

But Barkus didn't hear. Baby didn't hear.

They were asleep.

It had been a very long day.

TRADE ABOUT

There was a new dog next door.

It was Miss Daley's new dog.

"My sister gave me her dog because she has to travel," said Miss Daley.

"That's how I got Barkus!" I said. "From my Uncle Everton."

"Lucky us," said Miss Daley.

"Does Millie have toys?" I asked.

"A few old stuffed animals that smell bad. And my sister's sock so Millie won't miss her."

Barkus and Millie liked each other right away.

They played.

They swam in the lake.

They slept in the shade.

When they played inside our house, Baby
tried to play, too.

At first, Millie was afraid of the little animal
that wasn't a dog.

But soon they played together.

Some days Barkus went to Millie's house.

Some days Millie went to Barkus's house.

At night they both sat in the windows of their houses and looked across the yard at each other.

One morning Barkus came home with Millie's sock.

"You stole Millie's sock!" I said.

"Barkus borrowed it," said my mother. "I'm sure Millie will come over and take it back home."

But Millie didn't take her sock back home. She took the stuffed beaver with the flat shiny tail.

The next day Barkus brought home a worn stuffed rabbit with one ear.

"Borrowed," I told my mother.

Back and forth. Back and forth they went, trading toys.

Soon, all of Millie's toys were in Barkus's basket. And all of Barkus's toys were in Millie's toy tub.

"It's called a "trade about," said Miss Daley.

"A trade about," I said. "Maybe they'll trade about again."

And I was right.

That very night, when Barkus and Millie

looked out the windows at each other—

Barkus had his beaver.

Millie had her sock.

A trade about.

DOG DREAMS

A big storm was coming.

My mother bought food and ice and candles.

"Why ice and candles?" I asked.

"The electricity might go off when the winds come," said my father.

"That sounds scary," I said.

"Storms can be scary," said my mother. "But we'll be safe inside."

"Barkus doesn't look scared," I said.

Barkus and Baby lay in a curled-up heap.

"No, Barkus and Baby are not scared," said my mother.

It started to rain.

"You should take Barkus out now before it gets worse," said my father. He went outside to bring the lawn chairs inside.

Barkus didn't love rain. I had to push him outside.

"It's only rain, Barkus," I said.

But the rain came harder and the wind was
strong.

My father chased after a chair that was
blowing across the grass.

Miss Daley came out of her house with
Millie. She wore a rain hat and coat and
carried an umbrella.

Millie didn't love rain either.

Miss Daley's hat blew away and her umbrella turned inside out.

Then some shingles from Miss Daley's porch roof blew off above us. And a branch fell from our maple tree.

My father grabbed Miss Daley's arm.

We all ran to our house.

Miss Daley looked a little scared.

I was a little scared.

Miss Daley hung up her coat. I took off my shoes.

Barkus and Millie shook water over all of us.

That made Miss Daley smile.

"Come sit down," said my mother.

"You can stay with us until the storm is over," said my father.

"That's nice of you," said Miss Daley.

There was a sudden loud clap of thunder.

The lights went out.
My father lit the candles,
and my mother built a fire in the
fireplace.

The fire was cheerful. The dogs moved close to the fire and slept.

We ate sandwiches as the wind shook the house. We could hear small tree branches falling on the roof.

"I wonder why Baby and the dogs aren't scared," I said.

"They know we will take care of them," said Miss Daley.

"And they dream," she added.

Millie *yip-yip-yipped* in her sleep.

Barkus whined in his sleep. Then he moved his feet as if he were running.

"They are dreaming about chasing each other on a sunny day," said Miss Daley.

"I dream, too," I said. "Mostly good dreams.
Sunny days and ice cream."

"Like Barkus and Millie," said Miss Daley.
"They're having dog dreams."

"I like dog dreams," said my mother.

"Me, too," said my father.

"Me, too," I said.

As it turned out, that night we all dreamed
dog dreams.

And when we woke the next morning, the
wind and rain were gone.

And there was sun.